TINKER JIM

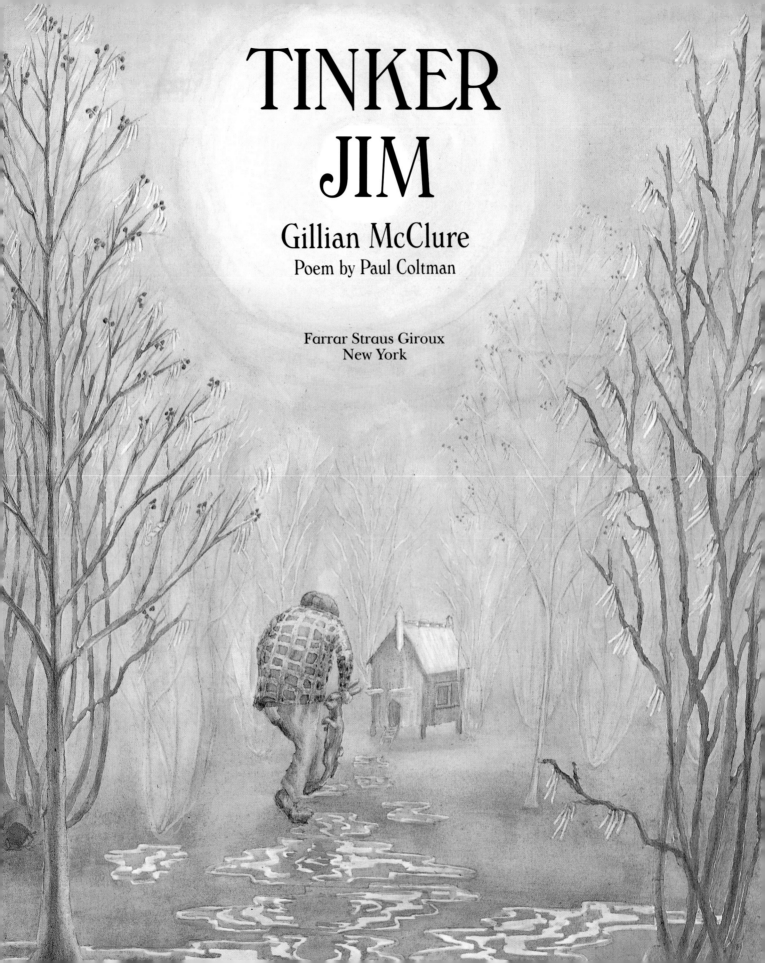

TINKER
JIM

Gillian McClure

Poem by Paul Coltman

Farrar Straus Giroux
New York

Jim lived in a chicken house
by a twist in Dead Mouse lane.
He squeezed in tight with fleas and mice.
When his feet got hot
he popped them out
and brought them back in for rain.

Tinker Jim was very thin.
He found his food where he could.
And when his pot had nothing in,
he went on the prowl
for a duck or a fowl
and cooked them alone in the wood.

His dad had taught Jim gypsy jobs:
He'd strip a stick and plait a basket,
mend pots, make pegs, trap jackdaw
                              squabs,

cure warts, catch moles,
make sugar-coated pills
from rabbit drops to sell at market.

But Jim was slack – he didn't work –
and fussy, too. He would not take
baked hedgehog, coots' eggs or roast rook.
And he didn't give a poop
for stinging nettle soup,
pignuts, puffballs, frog or snake.

One day Jim's buddy said to him,
"You's shrunk. You's gettin' thinner.
Yer bones show through,
    what didn't ought.
You should snoop around
for what can be found
to fatten up yer dinner."

Now, the Reverend Obadiah Delves
of Cudeleigh Rectory would give food
to "those less fortunate than ourselves."
Jim thought, "That's me.
I'll drop in and see
whether the Reverend's grub's any good."

But what he was offered opened his eye.
(He'd only got one and half an ear.)
"Reverend," he said with dignity,
"I can't eat **that**.
Give it back to the cat."
And he went off muttering, "Dear,
                        dear, dear."

Then he mooched and came to Cudeleigh
Towers,
where the Lady Millicent Mulberry Higg
walked in her garden fingering flowers.
She was pink and wore red.
"Cor! That one's well fed.
I bet me button she feeds like a pig."

Then out of the house a servant strolls,
nods to my Lady and goes to the garage.
But he didn't go in to polish the Rolls.
He soon came out
with a ten-pound trout,
a saddle of lamb and a sausage.

That night by the foxy light of the stars,
to a merry chorus of chicken,
Jim eased open the garage doors.
The freezer he found
was fifteen feet round,
far too ugly to stand in the kitchen.

And now his sooty cooking pot
gurgles with a toothsome stew:
with baked beans and bangers,
trotters and trout,
French fries and oysters,
dumplings and lobsters,
washed down with Lafitte '82.

Then Jim was ill. He thought he would die.
His mates, Snowy Parsons and
                    Moggie the Least,
watched as he closed his sad, red eye.
Then with a grin
they got tucking in
and finished the rest of the feast.

"I done it wrong, but if I lives,"
Jim thought, "I'll take me food in nips.
A willing stomach soon forgives."
Next night on his stump
with the moon as his lamp,
he sat down to pâté and chips.

In time Jim grew particular.
He liked a dry white wine with fish,
preferred to start with caviar;
no longer set snares
for rabbits and hares,
but carefully selected each dish.

Of course, by this time Jim had got
new pans and other gear.
Roses grew in his old black pot.
But his stinky clothes
offended his nose
and the mirror said, "Oh, dear!"

So he washed where he had never washed.
He scraped. He scrubbed above, beneath.
He chopped off his beard and emerged
                                    moustached,
used a flint as a file,
excavated a smile,
and practiced using a handkerchief.

Then the mirror said, "He's posh, a gent,
'cept for 'is togs 'e's stunnin'."
So back to Cudeleigh Towers he went.
Watched Cicely Wade,
her Ladyship's maid,
hang his Lordship's suit out for a sunning.

Next day he strolled down into town
in a grey pinstripe, trim and proper.
But as he stepped out of the
                    Goat and Crown,
" 'Ere, I want a word.
Yes, you. You 'eard."
He stood face to face with a copper.

Six months later Tinker Jim sat
at his chicken-house door. He was thinner
and had learned a bit more
about this and that.
But he'd found his pot,
old clothes, the lot,
and was cooking a rabbit for dinner.